Chapter One

Becky Harris liked her new school. She'd only been there a week. But already she'd made lots of friends.

She liked Imran. He was good at spelling.

She liked Carrie. She was good at maths.

She liked Daniel. He was good at drawing.

ALI IVES

My Dad is...

Illustrated by Georgie Birkett

MACDONALD YOUNG BOOKS

And she liked Susie. She was good at everything!

Becky also liked Mrs Darwin, their teacher. She was rather old, and rather wrinkly, but she seemed to be very kind.

Mrs Darwin wanted to know all about everyone in her class. So each week she asked them to write an essay about themselves.

Becky Harris
by Becky Harris

I like swimming and dancing and pony riding. And I love doing all these things with Sasha. She's my best friend. Sasha is four months older than me. She thinks that means she can boss me around. When she gets bossy, I just smile and ignore her. It works every time! I wish Sasha was at this school too. But, even though she isn't, I think I'm going to be very happy here.

This week Becky's class had to write a new essay. Mrs Darwin went up to the whiteboard and wrote in her large handwriting:

'My Dad is...'

"My Dad is... what?" said Imran, cheekily.

"A tree surgeon?" suggested Mrs Darwin. "An artist? A builder?"

"Does it have to be a job?" said Carrie.

"No," said Mrs Darwin. "Your dad
might not have a job. You could
write, 'My Dad is... my best friend!' "

"My Dad is... a couch potato!" said Imran, giggling. "That's what my mum always says!"

"Imran – *really*!" Mrs Darwin gave Imran one of her looks and walked over to his desk. He was going to get a telling off now!

The lunch-time bell rang as Becky stared at the whiteboard. My Dad is...! She thought about it long and hard.

This was going to be difficult.

It wasn't that she didn't like writing. She did.

MY DAD IS...

It wasn't that she couldn't spell.
She could.

The problem was far greater than that:

BECKY DIDN'T HAVE A DAD!

Chapter Two

Mrs Darwin hadn't finished telling the class about their essay when the bell rang. But she had to wait until lunch was over before she could say:

"Of course it doesn't have to be 'My Dad'. You could write about your step-dad, your uncle, or even your grandad! Any of those will do."

After all, Mrs Darwin knew that not everyone had a dad.

"Now, if no one has any more questions, I'll expect your essays on my desk on Friday morning."

Friday morning! Becky didn't have long, and she still didn't know what to write!

She didn't have a step-dad, an uncle or a grandad either. Her essay would be the shortest in the class!

Then Becky had a brilliant idea! She would make up a dad.

It was just a story, after all. And she did like writing stories. So how hard could it be?

That night after school Becky tried to picture her dad.

She didn't want a fat dad.

Or a bald dad.

Or an old dad.

In the end Becky decided that he would be very tall, and very sporty, with lots and lots of thick dark hair.

Just like hers.

He wouldn't have a beard.

And he wouldn't wear glasses either!

Sorted!

Now she had a dad!

Suddenly she laughed at herself.

A name!

Her dad would need a name!

Becky's mind went blank. She couldn't think of a single name!

So Becky asked her mum.

"Which boys' names do you like?" she asked as she ate her tea.

"I don't know," said her mum. "I've never really thought about it before."

"Well, if I had a brother," said Becky, "what would you call him?"

"Aah – that's easy," said her mum.

21

Benjamin! It was your grandad's name."

Becky smiled.

Now she had a name!

Chapter Three

So, Becky knew what her dad looked like. And what he was called. All he needed now was a job! She wondered what kind of jobs dads did.

The next day Becky asked her new friends about their dads.

"Mine's a doctor," said Carrie.

"Mine's a chef," said Daniel.

"Mine sells photocopiers," said Imran.

"Mine's an actor," said Susie.

Luckily, no one asked Becky what kind of job her dad did!

That night after school Becky got out her pencil and exercise book and started to write.

My Dad is... a doctor
by Becky Harris

My dad has a very important job.
He saves peoples lives. He works in
a hospital and he helps make all sorts
of people better. He looks after old
people who can't hear very well, and
ladies that are having babies. When
someone visits him they are called
a patient. My dad likes nearly all of
his patients, except the ones that
shout at him. I can't understand
why anyone would want to shout
at my dad. Especially if he is
trying to help them.

Becky re-read her essay.

It was no good. She couldn't picture her dad as a doctor. He would have to spend all his time working, and she'd never get to see him. That wouldn't do!

She tore the page out of the book and decided to start again.

27

My Dad is... an actor
by Becky Harris

My dad is an actor. I think he's
very good, but he doesn't think so. My
dad goes to lots of auditions. That's
when you try and get the part. Mum
says he doesn't get very many.
Sometimes you can see my dad on
TV. He doesn't have big parts, but
he's been a patient in a bed, and a man
in a pub, and a farmer in a field.
I've taped all his TV programmes
but I've never seen him act on the
stage. Yet. He says I will one day
soon. Mum says, I'll be lucky!

Becky was very pleased about the 'Mum' bits. They were just the kind of things her Mum would say!

That night Becky went to bed tired, and happy. Her make-believe dad was almost real!

Chapter Four

The next evening Becky decided that she didn't want her dad to be an actor. People might ask too many questions! And they might want to see the tapes. She thought about crossing that bit out, but then her essay would be far too short.

She would have to think of another job. Something less exciting. Something BORING!

My Dad is... a photocopier salesman by Becky Harris.

My dad has a very boring job. You wouldn't want to know about it. It would bore you. It bores me. And my mum.

Becky sat back and looked at the page. She was very pleased that she'd mentioned her mum again. After all, her mum deserved a mention. She did everything other people's mums *and* dads did. And she never complained.

Photocopiers copy paper. That's all they do. And my dad sells them to anyone who wants them.

This was getting tricky. What kind of people needed photocopiers? Becky asked her mum.

Hospitals, offices, banks, schools and prisons all use photocopiers. I don't need one. Neither does my mum. Or my gran.

Becky decided that selling photocopiers was a very boring job. So boring, in fact, that she tore up her piece of paper and started again.

Writing about her dad wasn't easy. It couldn't be too interesting, otherwise people would want to know more. But if she had to have a dad, she didn't want him to be too boring, either. Then he'd be no fun at all! Becky was beginning to wonder what she could do.

Chapter FIVE

My Dad is... a chef
by Becky Harris

My dad is a chef and he works
in a restaurant.

Becky's mum liked watching TV
programmes about food. So Becky
thought that this one should be
quite easy to write.

Becky chewed the end of her pencil.
What kind of food did he cook?

Was it Italian food?

Or Indian?

Or Chinese?

Or French? Well, she didn't want to have to eat frogs' legs or snails!

But Italian food? That was different! Becky loved pizzas.

He works in an Italian restaurant and he cooks pizzas and lasagne and spaghetti bolognese. I like his pizzas best. They have a big thick crust and lots of cheese and pepperoni.

Becky pictured herself in her dad's restaurant, surrounded by hundreds of pizzas. She would go there at least once a week. And she'd be allowed to eat as much as she could!

Becky licked her lips. She was getting hungry. She went into the kitchen to see what was for tea.

"Mum, if you worked in a restaurant," she said, "would you cook nice meals for me when you got home?"

Becky's mum laughed.

"No," she said. "I wouldn't! I'd probably give you beans on toast."

'But when my dad gets home from work,' she continued to write, 'he's tired of cooking. So my mum cooks all my meals. Sometimes we have pizza. Sometimes we have chips. But when she's tired we just have beans on toast.'

Becky put down her pencil and sat back, thoughtfully.

She rather liked the idea of her dad
being a chef. It was better than being
a doctor, or an actor, and it was
much, much better than being
a photocopier salesman!

So finally she'd made up her mind.
If she had to have a dad, he would
be a chef!

Finally Becky was ready to hand in her essay. And just in time, too! Mrs Darwin wanted to read them all the very next day.

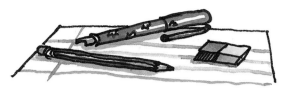

Chapter Six

Later on Friday afternoon Mrs Darwin
said she was going to read one of the
essays out in class. She thought it
was brilliant. And she wanted
everyone else to hear it too.

No one knew which essay
Mrs Darwin was going to read.
She perched on the edge of her desk
and smiled.

My Dad is... my Mum!
by Becky Harris

I haven't got a dad or a step-dad
or an uncle or a grandad. But I
have got my mum. I think she
does everything any dad would do.
And more! She does all
the things that
mums do too.

We go swimming. We play games. She's teaching me to paint, and we're even building a new rabbit hutch together. She helps with my school work (although she doesn't know about this essay) and she never ever yells and shouts at me. My mum also goes to work. She doesn't like her job very much. She says it's boring. But my mum isn't boring. She could never be boring! She's the best mum, and the best dad, in the world!

Becky sat in her seat and blushed. She had been going to give Mrs Darwin the essay about her make-believe dad. Then, suddenly she'd realized, she did have a dad.

She had a mum, and a dad, all rolled into one!